BOOKTOPUS

Princess CASTLE Activity Book

Amazing book for amazing kids!

Match each object to its shadow.

Trace the path to help the mermaid reach the pearl.

Trace the picture and colour it beautifully.

Look at the pattern carefully and name what will come next.

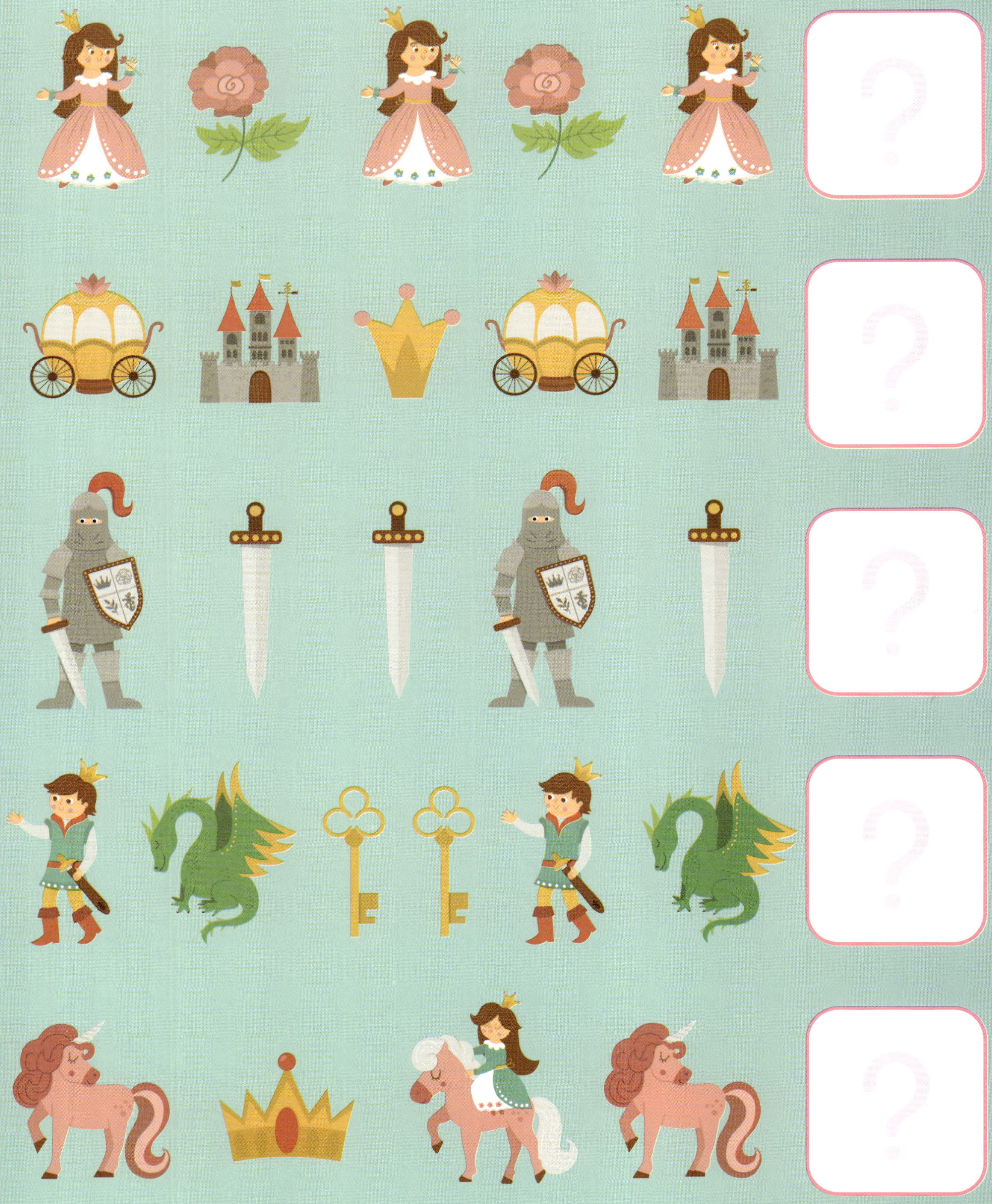

Circle the identical princesses.

Count and write the number of objects in each box.

Look at the objects in each row and try to trace, then draw, and colour the objects as shown.

Count and write how many times each object is appearing below.

Trace the path and help the princesses reach their shell.

Circle the castle with blue flags.

Match the beautiful princess to her correct shadow.

Draw and Colour the mermaid princess as shown.

Trace the pattern in each row.

Draw and Colour the other half of the castle.

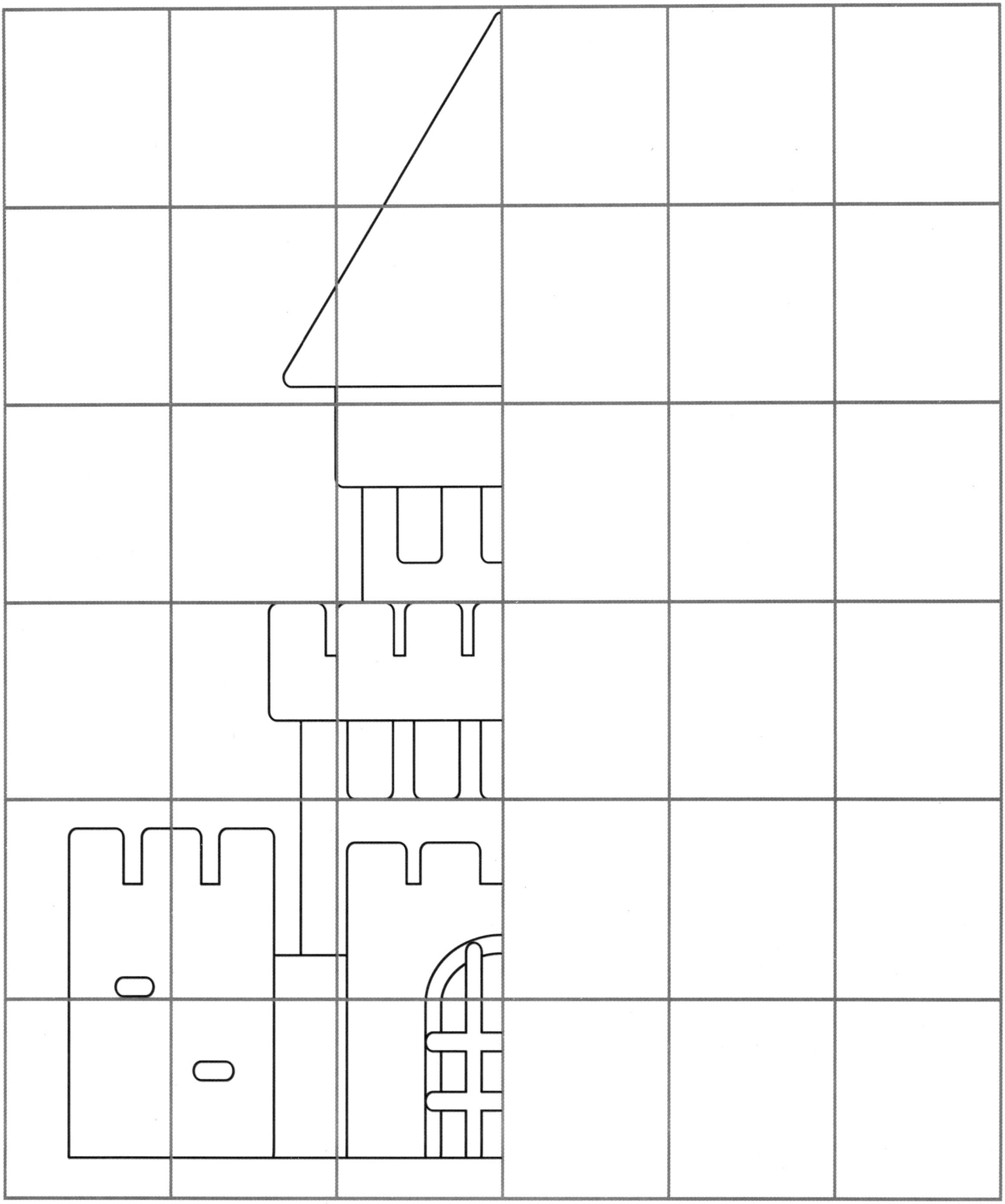

Solve the picture sums.

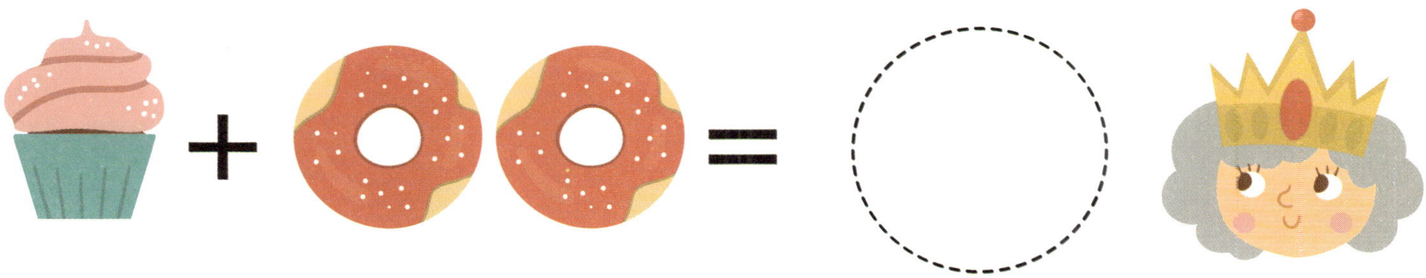

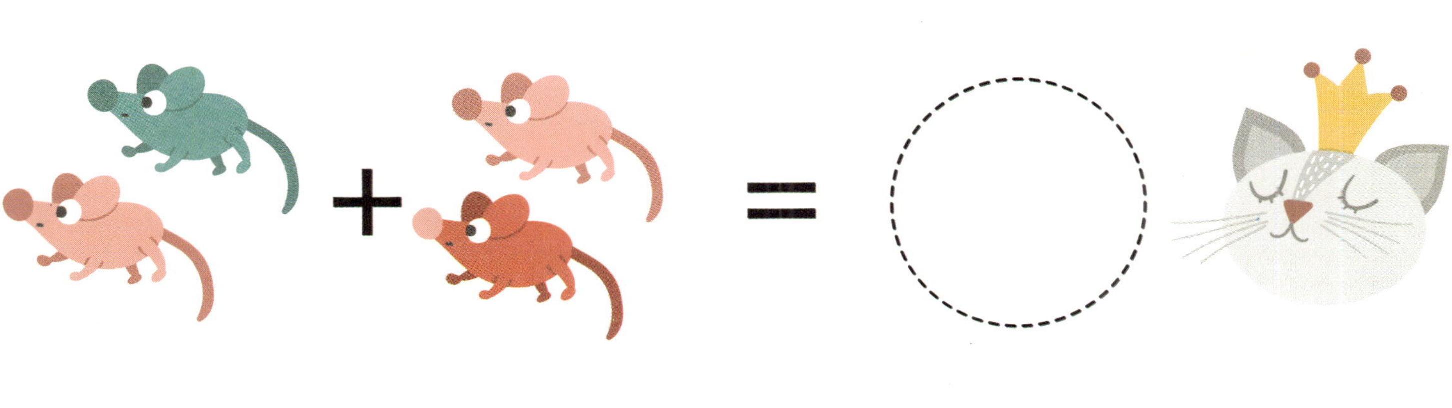

Count and write how many times each object is appearing below.

Colour the princess as shown.

Match each princess to her bellies.

Number the puzzle pieces in the correct order to complete the picture.

Doodle and Colour some more elements related to a princess.

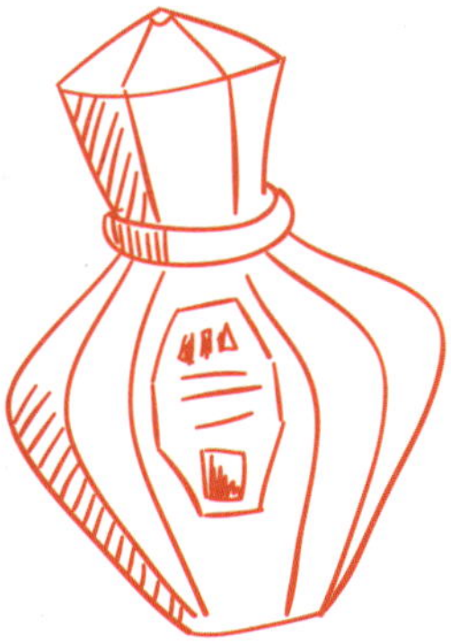

Look carefully and circle the mermaid that looks different.

Spot and circle the differences between the two princesses.

Find and circle the different looking group.

Trace all the butterflies and colour them in bright colours.

Circle the smallest object in each row.

Colour the picture according to the given Colour Code.

1

2

3

4

5

6

What comes next? Observe and match to the answer. One is done for you.

Circle the odd one out.

Match each princess to her shadow.

Follow the given direction code to take the princess to her chariot.

Find the key that will unlock the gate.

Count and write how many times each object is appearing below.

Princess CASTLE Activity Book

BOOKTOPUS
An imprint of HarperCollins *Publishers* India
www.harpercollins.co.in
HarperCollinsIN